One morning, Lucas woke up and felt
something was missing in his life...

He wanted to have a really wonderful friend.
And so he decided, on such a wonderful day,
that he would go out and find one.

Lucas lived not very far from a popular beach. Surely, finding a really wonderful friend among all the people there would be easy.
He looked and he looked... yet not one person in this overcrowded place could be considered in the slightest.

How much does two scoops of ice cream cost? Do you see the children who are building a sandcastle? And the man doing yoga?

Lucas knew of some offices nearby. Having a friend
in business would be pretty cool, he thought.
But he found that office workers are always busy,
and they're not always on the lookout for friends.

Oops, someone spills coffee! Where is the coffee machine?

Lucas went off to a rock concert, where he was surrounded
by heaps of rock fans and guitars. But though he tried
to talk over the loud music, it became clear that he would
never get to know anyone amidst all this noise.

Do you see the couple who poses for a photo?
And the man who shouts?

I should look in a quieter environment, Lucas thought,
so he popped into a pet shop. But Lucas couldn't find even one
really wonderful friend. In the end, all he could do was help the
workers in the store who told him about their best friends.

Can you spot the chameleon, even though it's camouflaged?
Who carries the food bag with a hole in it?

Then he went to his old school from a few years back... maybe a teacher could be his new best friend? This idea, however, was totally absurd! If there was ever a person with no time for friends, it was a school teacher during his break.

Who plays with the paper airplanes, and who draws something with chalk?
Can you find the one who lost his glasses?

Nobody ever said it was going to be simple.
True friendships have never been easy to make, thought Lucas.
Yet, he always seemed to be near crowds of nice and interesting people.
Why can't I become really best friends with just one of them?

Can you find the gecko? And the mouse?

CRASH

Lucas slowly felt a frustration bubbling up inside him, and he urgently needed to lift his spirits. So, he went to a leisure park. Maybe he could find an adventurous kind of friend there? Everyone at the park, however, was just there for fun, and not a single person seemed to be interested in him.

Where can you buy cotton candy? And what's that piece of paper lying on the carousel? Does it look familiar?

Suddenly, an idea dawned upon him! Lucas needed someone who was new to the city, someone he could take to see all the sights. And where was he most likely to find that kind of person? At the airport, of course! But when Lucas arrived there, it was swarming with nervous travelers carrying heavy suitcases. Nobody finds new friends in such a hectic atmosphere!

Be careful! A pickpocket is about – can you spot him?

MILAN 16:15
LONDON 16:25
PARIS 17:00
BERLIN 17:15

Lucas remembered that a circus had come to town a few weeks ago,
so he decided to take a look. Certainly, people in circuses
would never carry heavy suitcases or even be in a bad mood.
But it's really difficult to get noticed in a circus
if you can't perform dangerous tricks.

Three people have lost their glasses! Can you find them?

He even tried his luck in the middle of a few traffic jams,
but all the people there were frustrated and unfriendly.
Lucas was beginning to think his search might be pointless.
Finding a new, really wonderful friend
was much harder than he had thought.

Can you find the circus car in the traffic? And the
baggage trolley – whoops, what is that doing here?

Lucas loved birthday parties... and when he learned that
one was happening nearby, he made his way there immediately.
But he ended up paying more attention to the birthday cake
than to the people around him.

Can you find the birthday girl?

After the birthday party, Lucas went to his favorite park.
There was a lot going on and he had a lot of fun, but there
was no trace of his really special friend.

Can you find a dog on a skateboard? And the tourist
with a camera and a guide book?

Near the park was a peaceful lake,
where there were some rowing boats.
Sadly, though, Lucas found that all the people
there seemed to have a very best friend already.
That is to say, everyone except him.

Where are the duck and dog couples?

Such a tough day! Lucas had to rest up and eat something.
He went to a cafe and, between sandwiches and salads,
some interesting potential friends arrived on the scene.
But Lucas only seemed to notice the sandwiches and salads!

What are the dogs eating?

Lucas now had a full stomach and felt much better, so he went to the botanical garden. It was so beautiful there that he was determined to bring the most wonderful friend of all time to this place as soon as he found him or her. But the best friend was nowhere to be seen.

How many firs are there?

On the way home he found himself at a street party.
It was full of friendly, good natured revelers.
Lucas stayed there for a while, but by now he was so tired
that he made off without even noticing a girl
who would have loved to become his very best friend.

Can you spot the girl?

Bruno is never cold. Or have you ever seen him in warmer clothes?

Carl Croco is a typical businessman. His motto is: never leave the house without a suitcase.

Mia likes Lucas instantly! She'd love to be his best friend!

Lucas arrived home exhausted and without a single wonderful friend. Nevertheless, he went happily to bed. Today had been a big adventure, and Lucas had encountered many new and extraordinary people.

The enthusiastic gardener George always carries his pruner with him.

Ramon, Manuel and Pepe come from Mexico and are always singing love songs. Now and then, one of them loses his hat.

Wild Zora is unstoppable.

The nice waitress is called Rebecca. She likes Lucas, too!

Although he looks a bit dangerous, Rocky is a very friendly guy. Could it be that he is playing an instrument?

There are only a few dogs as well-read as Buster. Where did Lucas meet him for the first time?

You can go bananas with Lisa and Lucy. The inseparable sisters are constantly losing their glasses!

With his in-line skates Mike is blazing fast. Do you know what his girlfriend's name is?

And who knows, maybe one day he will find the special person he was seeking?

Can you find all of these people on the cover of the book? Only one is missing - which one is that?

This is Grandpa Miller. You have to be careful around him, though!

What does Akhmed have in all these suitcases? Did you notice what he uses his luggage for at the lake?

Stupid August is not stupid at all. He loves birthday parties, because he can joke around with all the kids there.

Jorgos scolds all the time!

Where did Lucas meet Wilfred? It's obvious, right?

Get Stuck In!

This book is not just a story about Lucas, the boy who looks everywhere for a really wonderful friend. It also contains many seek and find games.

You could play the games with your own best friend or with a whole party of friends.

You can also make up your own puzzle questions. If there's a bunch of you, then you can ask your questions in turn. Whoever comes up with the answer first gets a point, and then whoever gets the most points at the end is the winner.

Here are some ideas for your seek and find games:

- I see something you can't see ... What is it?

- Look at a picture for a while, then close the book and answer questions without looking at the picture. For example, how many people are in the band at the concert? What are the colors on the page? Where can Lucas be found? How many amplifiers are there?

- Take a guess at how many animals are in the pet shop. Guess first and then count them!

- Find Lucas and all the people who follow him. But take care! They increase in number, and with every page a new person shows up.

Have fun seeking and finding!